For Nico, with love, for revealing to me the
secret that there are princesses alive in museums.

Marina García

Born in Buenos Aires, Argentina, one autumn morning
last century. From an early age she liked going
around telling stories and doing sketches.
When she grew up, she became an architect, which
she liked a lot. But not long ago, she left the building
world to devote herself to writing and illustrating
children's books which she likes even more.
And it all started several years ago when she came
to visit Spain, the land of her grandparents, whose
magic trapped her. She didn't want to go back...
Now she lives in Seville with her small son Nicolás
and has published several books on art and travel
for children.

ediciones
SerreS

Mateo at the Museum

A trip to the Prado

Text and illustrations

Marina Garcia

Photographic Acknowledgments
© Museo del Prado, Madrid 2003
© Joaquín Sorolla, VEGAP, Barcelona 2003

Original Title: Mateo de paseo por... El Museo del Prado

Translation: Luke Stobart

Text and illustrations
© 2003 Marina García Gurevich
lucanor@teleline.es

© 2003 Ediciones Serres, S. L.
Muntaner, 391 – 08021 – Barcelona
www.edicioneserres.com

English rights for Spain only

First Edition, 2003
First Reprint, 2005

ISBN: 84-8488-071-0

Editorial design: Estudio Marina García

"Come on. Get dressed quickly!" said my grandma, excitedly. "I'm going to take you to a very special place with treasures belonging to kings and queens from many, many years ago... And you¨ll even find princes and princesses!".
I had a quick look in my wardrobe for something that could give me a "princely" look for this special occasion: a hat, a mask, my Spiderman suit...I tried everything. I even put a little shoe polish on my face to look like one of the Three Kings...But it was no good. I looked like the same old Mateo!

"Oh no! Costumes: no way!" said my grandma on seeing me, and she made me put on my usual jersey and jeans. "In the museum you¨ll see lots of people painted with their customary clothes..." she started explaining as we were walking along, "some smarter than others but each wearing the clothes of their era."

"Did you say "MUSEUM!!??

"Of course. In the Prado Museum there are princes and princesses but also hunters, dogs and horses and a lots more to be discovered," she added while we climbed some immense stairs to a door that said it belonged to a gentleman named Goya...

I thought that the gentleman would be by his door, but I couldn't see him. It seems he wasn't the Knight surrounded by columns right at the entrance to the museum either. Then grandma took my hand and led me through a wide and very long room where lots of pictures were hanging.

"First of all, we'll visit Princess Margarita," she said excitedly. "You'll see, she's such a pretty princess!..."

"Here she is," said grandma, while she sat down and untied the laces of her shoes to rest a little. A girl with long, blond hair was looking at me from an enormous painting. All of a sudden, the painter stopped painting, a young woman with curly hair looked at me out of the corner of her eye, a gentleman stopped still by the door and even a couple stuck their heads out to spy through the mirror at the back. They were all looking at me!

Well, that's what it seemed like...Then some very strange things started to happen.

Las Meninas or the Family of Philip IV
Diego Velázquez

"I'm leaving. That's it; I'm getting really bored here!" shouted the blond girl. And without further ado, she took an enormous jump out the painting. She was wearing a huge dress adorned with flowers and some shoes with really big soles. It looked like she was floating on air!

"And what are you doing with that silly look on your face? Have you never seen a princess escape from a painting before?" she said.

"My name's Mateo," I stammered, feeling a little bewildered. "And yours?"

"I'm Princess Margarita!" she answered proudly and added "my dad is King Felipe IV and Queen Mariana is my mum. And now the only thing I want is enjoy myself and go for a wander outside. Are you coming?"

I go away!!!

Shhh!

"To really enjoy yourselves, you should escape through the window behind my back," suggested a man with very long curls and a striped cap. "I promise I won't tell anybody that I've seen you," he whispered.

He also told us that he was called Dürer and that he had done the painting of himself when he was a young man.

"Come on, Mateo, this'll be brillant!" Margarita winked at me, grabbed my hand and before I could say anything she made me take a big jump though the window. But...What would be waiting on the other side?

Self-portrait
Albrecht Dürer

Fruits that looked like machines, a knife between two ears, a couple inside a bubble...Even an egg-shaped man!

This was the closest thing to a nightmare.

OHhhh!

"This garden doesn't look anything like the gardens in my palace," exclaimed Margarita sirprised, while the bubble drifted around her dress. Nobody noticed us and everyone seemed happy doing their own thing. Only the man with the egg-shaped body turned his head towards us, making the dancers that were on him fall off. They nearly fell into the water!

The Garden of Delights
Hieronymus Bosch

"We are having a fantastic time! We eat what we want, dance through the air, shoot arrows and play hide-and-seek," a crowd of angels said in unison, as they flapped their tiny wings. They fluttered around us and took us into the air.

We have a fantastic time!

We shoot arrows

We dance

We eat

Or play hide-and-seek

Up in the sky, some danced to a heavenly beat. Below on the grass, the chubbiest and most mischievous ones had enormous fun: they danced, played and went up and down trees throwing apples from them. A young woman was trying yo pick one but it was very difficult and she nearly fell.

A smiling angel offered us the reddest one and we nibbled them on the way to the hill where the laughter was coming from...

The Immaculate Conception
"of Soult"
Bartolomé Esteban Murillo

Offering to Venus
Titian

Ha! ha!

"Come on, Mateo! It looks like they are having great fun," said Margarita and we took off to follow them... What could be such fun?

Do we look like giants?

Let me through!

Neigh!

Lying down on wet sand is the wickedest!

Ha-ha!

"Shall we play at being giants?" asked the boy with the hat and red jacket.
Margarita said no: "a princess doesn't do silly things!"
But then she changed her mind and I had to carry her on my back.
Wow, princesses can be quite heavy with those dresses!
"It's a lot more fun to ride horses and go hunting," shouted someone that came
galloping towards us, nearly squashing us with his brown horse.
"Careful, Baltasar Carlos!" shouted Margarita, who seemed to know him quite well.

The Little Giants
Francisco de Goya y Lucientes

Baltazar Carlos on Horseback
Diego Velázquez

Splasshh!!

Farther along, some children were lying on the seashore throwing handfuls of sand at each other.

"This does look fun! Help me take off my clogs because I want to walk on the wet sand" ordered Margarita. I helped her and even carried her shoes for her. After all she is a princess. Margarita held her skirt to her and we began to jump from here to there until we heard the music that the waves washed onto the beach...

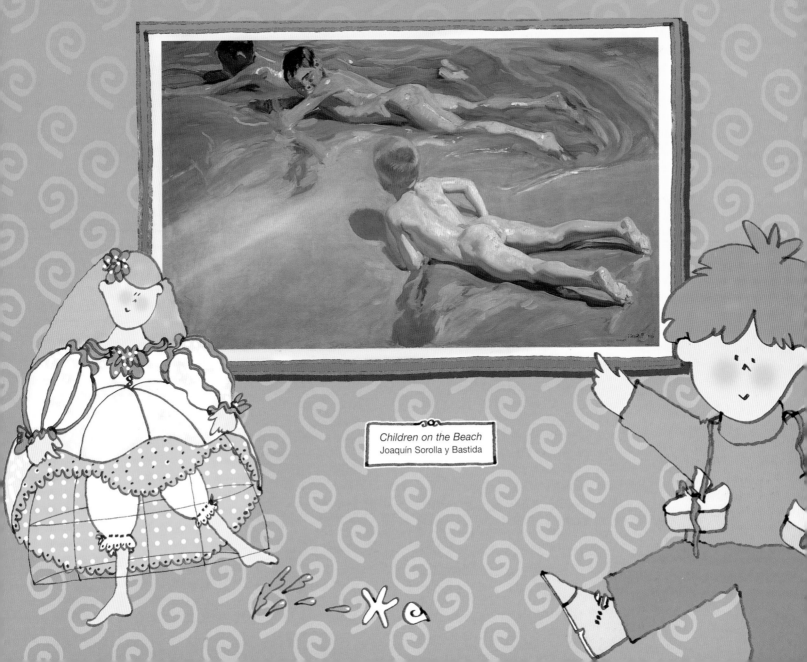

Children on the Beach
Joaquín Sorolla y Bastida

Tick!-tock!

Clocks, violins, cellos, zithers, clavichords, trumpets, parrots, toucans and drums...

Tick!-tock!

The music was drowning everything, but the child with the flute only heard his own tune...

We started a great uproar. We played drums and Margarita even felt inspired to play the double bass. But the child didn't even look at us.
"What are you doing here so alone?" asked Margarita intrigued. "Don't you get bored?"
"I'm not alone or bored," the boy responded without taking his eyes off the flutes.
"My music and my friend keep me company." Beside him was a white and woolly sheep. It was nibbling the grass and moving its head.

Idyll
Mariano Fortuny i Marsal

The music led us to an inmense room. There in the middle were a woman and a child.
They were singing accompanied by several animals.
"Listen carefully and dance to the sounds of all the musical instruments and
the exotic birds," said the young woman, turning her glance towards us.
"And pay special attention to the tick-tocking of the clocks!"

Allegory of Hearing
Jan Brueghel de Velours

And off we went dancing and spinning around and around until...

A fluffy pink **cloud** came towards us and invited us to climb aboard.

In the field and on the banks of the river we could see a large amount of people...

"Come on down and join the celebration!" said the lady with the parasol when she saw us.

"A party! How I like parties," shrieked Margarita excitedly.

But...what were they celebrating there?

Hey!

"Come to the san Isidro festival and I'll paint a portrait of you there!" suggested a gentleman who was painting all the colours of the party on a board. Some small strokes here, a few dabs there and an enormous fluffy pink cloud in the sky.

Margarita told me that the man was the painter Francisco de Goya!

I asked her if he was the same Mr Goya as that of the museum entrance. She told me she had no idea.

The maja dressed in white gave Margarita her parasol, making her very happy.

The Shooting of May Third 1808
Francisco de Goya y Lucientes

¡Baangg!, ¡Bang!...There were shots nearby

Woof! Woof!

There was barking everywhere

Zzzz.... Zzzz...

We quickly hid.
"Shh!" said the boy with the shotgun. "You'll scare away the deer!"
His dog, wich was sleeping next to him, didn't make a sound!

¡W oof! Woof!

In the distance there was a terrible uproar. The dogs barked madly behind the deer while the hunters trailed them.

A scared dog watched the situation half sunken in his hiding place.

"This dog doesn't seem to like the hunt so much" said Margarita with a.know-it-all face. "If you don't believe me, ask Baltasar Carlos. He knows a lot about these things."

Perro semihundido
Francisco de Goya

W Ooff.

Woof!

Wooff!

The boy with the hunter's suit and cap smiled proudly when he heard his name.
It was the boy who nearly rode over us with his horse!
"One day, as well as being King, I'm going to be a good hunter," he declared, while
he held his shotgun tightly.
"Ha-ha! Well, you'll have to find a more alert dog," laughed Margarita pointing to
the pointer snoring at his side.
The greyhound, which was hidden, smiled without moving an inch.

Baltasar Carlos Hunter
Diego Velázquez

Bang! Bang!

Ready...Aim...Fire!...

We're in front of a firing squad!

Margarita nearly fainted and it was my turn to be the brave one.

"One day I'm going to paint this horrible killing," whispered a recognisable voice.

It was Goya. He was hiding on the same side as us, spying with his telescope.

An enormous lantern lit up the grey-uniformed soldiers who were aiming at a group of men. We were petrified...

The Shootings of May Third
1808
Francisco de Goya

"Let´s go! Follow me, quick. I´ll get you out of here..."

Said the young man who seemed to be in a great rush. He was running along throwing golden apples around him. "Don't even think about touching them!" he exclaimed, guessing our intentions. "They are a trap for Atalanta. She'll stop to pick them up and I shall win the race!" he added, and off he ran with his large scarf flapping in the wind.

"

Just then she appeared, running with her long hair and covered with a blue-toned cloth.. "Hippomenes won't beat me!" she said, sure that she was the fastest. "Neither his traps nor his tricks will make me lose this race, or my name is not Atalanta!" Margarita took off her clogs to run more comfortably and I had to carry them again...Well, princesses can be like that.

We ran a distance with them until some other people came out to meet us...

Hippomenes and Atalanta
Guido Reni

"Where are you rushing to?" one of them asked in a very serious voice.

¡Oh!, no!

princesses mustn´t behave like that," said a woman.

"You should take it a little more easily," added another calmly.

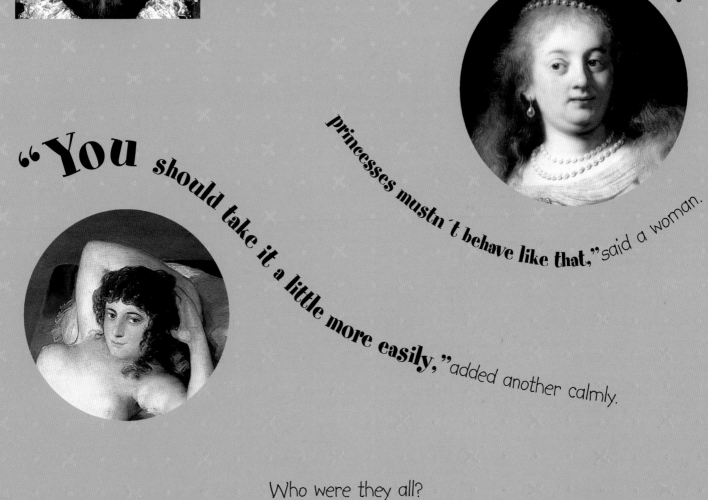

Who were they all?
Margarita, quarrelsome as always, replied that nobody would tell her, a princess,
what she should or shouldn´t do. She was really angry!

Hmmmm!

"My, my, there's no need to get so mad, young lady," said the woman lying on enormous white cushions as she stretched out.

She was watching us with the most mysterious smile on her face. She seemed happy to be here doing nothing. "as you can see, I've been here posing for a great many hours, while Goya does several portraits of me," she clarified. She didn't seem particulary worried. "In the one he did before I wore more clothes. Now I'm not but I'very relaxed about it!"

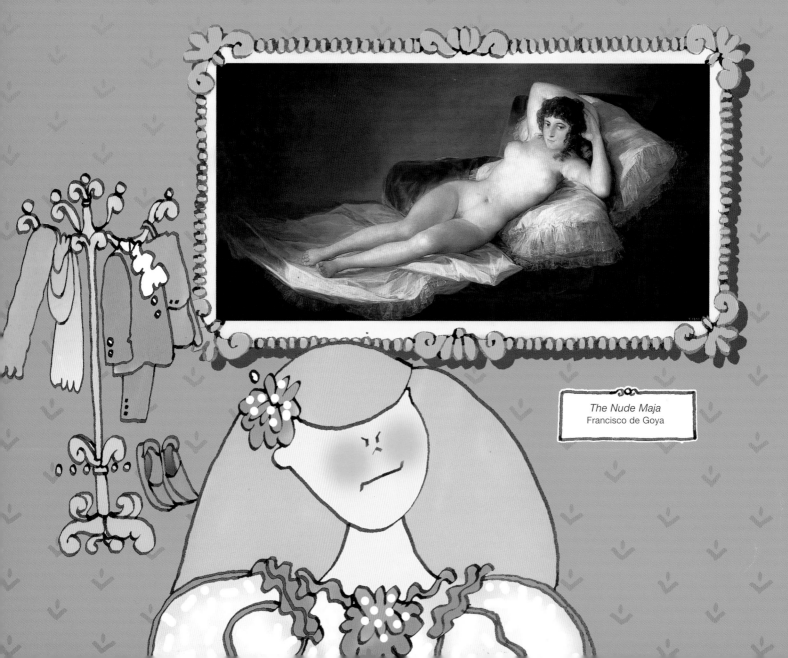

The Nude Maja
Francisco de Goya

If you want to know what relaxed is, just look at me! I'm going to drink this beverage without uttering a word," added a plump woman emerging from the shadows. the golden light lit her up, highlighting her luxurious dress and jewellery.

"To my mind, posing naked isn't appropiate for a lady," interrupted a very tall gentleman, placing his hand on his chest."

"How elegant it is to dress in dark suits and a collar as tall and white as mine."

Artemis
Rembrandt Harmensz Van Rijn

The Knight with His Hand on His Breast
Domenikos Theotokopoulos

¡ClinK!... ¡clank!

Ahh! Ahh!

ClinK!.... Clunk! The coins clinked as they fell...

Here nobody was taking any notice of us.
The people were all concentrating hard on their jobs.
Then we went near, without making any noise, to spy on them...

The man with a large belly yelled, tied to his chair.

"You'd be better off if we take off the stone that is on your head," explained another man, who carried a tin funnel on his. "These people are all mad," said the mean-looking man with the enormous hat. "I spend my time doing much more serious things, such as exchanging and collecting coins."

"Me too!" I said, keenly. "Can I take one for my collection?" "Nooo!" he and his wife answered in unison, without taking their eyes off the scales that were weighing the coins.

The Cure of Folly or The Stone Operation
Hieronymus Van Aeken Bosch

The Money changer and His Wife
Marinus Claeszon van Reymerswaele

Princess Margaritaaaa!

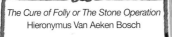

"Margaritaaaaaaa!" shouted the dawrf as he ran towards us.
He was very concerned. That was strange for a dwarf, as they were usually so much fun. But at the same time, he did seem very funny.
"Miss Margarita," he said a little irritated, "you should go back to Mr diego Velázquez's studio. Everyone is waiting for you. Even the King and Queen are getting impatient." having said that, he sat in his picture and there he stayed. He was half worn out, with his legs spread out and showing the minuscule soles of his shoes...SHOES?? Margarita suddenly remembered that she wasn't wearing hers. And I had to help her put them back on...

Don Sebastián de Morra
Diego Velázquez

I'd better go now, Mateo," stammered Margarita. "I don't want to get on the wrong side of my parents and I've already had a great day." Then she took a big jump and shot into a picture containing many people with the most royal clothes, jewellery and faces imaginable. And then the trouble started...

"Go on, get out!" yelled the boy with the colorful red suit. "You're squahing me!"

"There's no room for you here," added another girl hugging her mother. The mother glared furiously at Margarita...

To top it all off, in the midst of so much chaos, the baby started crying.

What a disaster!

Shhhh!

"As King Charles IV, and head of this family, it seems clear to me that there is one to many and that is you, young lady" stated the man with the white wig, who shone like a real King. He wore lots of medals and a blue and white band across his chest.

Margarita was red with shame and couldn't utter a word...

She had got the wrong painting...THIS was not HER family!

"Go out this way!" whispered a familiar voice, wich was in fact Goya's. He was painting the family's portrait, hidden behind them all.

Margarita tiptoed away. A young woman turned her head when she saw her but just winked and didn't say a word to anybody.

La familia de Carlos IV
Francisco de Goya

"Maargaritaaa!!! Where are you?"
I asked intrigued. With such a fuss going on I had lost my friend.
"MATEOOOO!!!!! Are you listening to what I'm saying?"
My grandma's voice snapped me away from my thughts in a flash.
"Look at the girl at the centre of the painting," added grandma. "Look how still
she stands while they paint her. She almost seems to float on air!"

"Of course. It's because of her clogs,"
I said, remembering my friend's enormous shoes.
"B e c a u s e   o f   w h a t ? ?" asked grandma, astounded.
"Because of the shoes she's wearing with the enormous soles," I mumbled
smiling. I didn't tell her anything else.
I was afraid she might say that I invent the most incredible stories!
I think I heard Margarita tittering as we left...

Tock! -Tock!

What I'm sure of is that she winked at me and tapped on the floor twice with her heels to say goodbye. We left the museum through the Goya door, the same one we came in through. But Goya wasn't there this time either.

Well, it doesn't matter because now I know where to find him and my friend Margarita. Whenever I want!...

Tock! - Tock!

With M for Mateo

When we left the museum, we went walking down the street called Paseo del Prado. Grandma told me it has that name because a long time ago it was a stream surrounded by pastures and fields... And now it has some enormous trees!

We crossed the Botanical Garden and then went down a street with stands filled with lots of books.
We had a peek in several and grandma bought me a book about a princess, as a souvenir from our trip to the museum...Then we took the underground back home.

Princesas
Pr
sas

I later made a collage on paper. I used postcards and tickets from the museum, some leaves that I found while we were walking, and a drawing of my friend Margarita as I remembered her. Then I pinned it to my bedroom wall so that everybody would know about my fantastic trip through the museum.

With M for Museum

1. *Las meninas or the Family of Philip IV,* Diego Velázquez (1656)/ 2. *Self-portrait,* Albrecht Dürer (1498)/

3. *The Garden of Earthly Delights,* Hieronymus Bosch (h.1505)/ 4. *Offering to Venus,* Titian (h.1518-1519)/

5. *The Immaculate Conception,* Bartolomé Esteban Murillo.(h.1678)/ 6. *The Little Giants,* Francisco de Goya (1791-92)/

7. *Baltasar Carlos on Horseback,* Diego Velázquez (1635)/ 8. *Children on the Beach,* Joaquín Sorolla (1910)/

9. *Allegory of Hearing,* Jan Brueghel de Velours (h.1617)/ 10. *Idyll,* Mariano Fortuny i Marsal (1868)/

11. *The Shootings of May Third 1808,* Francisco de Goya (1814)

In this picture gallery you will be able to recognise all the paintings appearing in Mateo and Princess Margarita's adventure that are in the Prado Museum.
Some are very big and others very small. Observe their real size and compare them with the height of the visitors in the drawings.
Had you imagined that some would be so large and others so small?

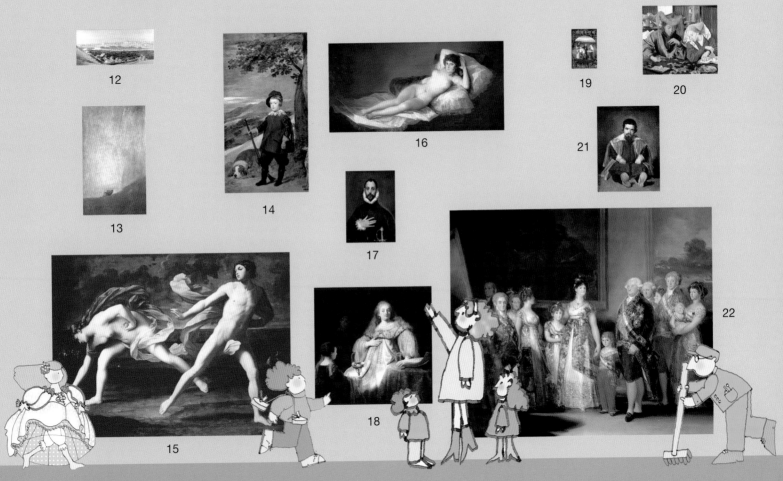

12. ***The Meadow of San Isidro,*** Francisco de Goya (1788)/ 13. ***Perro semihundido,*** Francisco de Goya (h.1820-1823)/ 14. ***Baltasar Carlos Hunter,*** Diego Velázquez (1635)/ 15. ***Hippomenes and Atalanta,*** Guido Reni (h.1630)/ 16. ***The Nude Maja,*** Francisco de Goya.(1798-1805)/ 17. ***The Knight with His Hand on His Breast,*** Domenicos Theotocopoulos (h.1578)/ 18. ***Artemis,*** Rembrandt Harmensz van Rijn (1634)/ 19.**The Cure of Folly or The Stone Operation,** Hieronymus Bosch (1910)/ 20. ***The Money Changer and His Wife,*** Marinus Claeszon van Reymerswaele (1539)/ 21. ***Don Sebastián de Morra,*** Diego Velázquez (1644)/ 22. ***The Family of Charles IV,*** Francisco de Goya (1800)